S0-AWV-600

um, Elizabeth.
eil Armstrong /

2006.
3305217841950
1   12/07/09

American Lives

Neil Armstrong

Elizabeth Raum

Heinemann Library
Chicago, Illinois

© 2006 Heinemann Library
a division of Reed Elsevier Inc.
Chicago, Illinois

Customer Service 888-454-2279
Visit our website at www.heinemannlibrary.com

All rights reserved. No part of this publication may
be reproduced or transmitted in any form or by
any means, electronic or mechanical, including
photocopying, recording, taping, or any information
storage and retrieval system, without permission in
writing from the publisher.

Designed by Joanna Hinton-Malivoire and
Q2A Creative

Printed in China by
WKT Company Limited

10 09 08 07 06
10 9 8 7 6 5 4 3 2 1

Library of Congress Cataloging-in-Publication Data
Raum, Elizabeth.
  Neil Armstrong / Elizabeth Raum.-- 1st ed.
    p. cm. -- (American lives)
  Includes bibliographical references and index.
  ISBN 1-4034-6938-5 (hc) -- ISBN 1-4034-6945-8
(pb)
  1. Armstrong, Neil, 1930---Juvenile literature. 2.
Astronauts--United States--Biography--Juvenile
literature. 3. Project Apollo (U.S.)--Juvenile
literature. 4. Space flight to the moon--Juvenile
literature. I. Title. II. Series.
  TL789.85.A75R3865 2005
  629.45'0092--dc22

                  2005006251

Acknowledgments
The author and publishers are grateful to the
following for permission to reproduce copyright
material: Alamy Images p. 10 (Andre Jenny);
Alamy Images/Transtock Inc. p. 8; Corbis p. 25;
Corbis/Bettmann cover, p. 16; Corbis/Hulton
Deutsche Collection p. 12; Corbis/Underwood &
Underwood p. 5; Getty Images p. 29; Getty
Images/Time-Life Pictures pp. 13, 19; NASA
pp. 24, 27; NASA/Ames Research Center p. 17;
NASA/Dryden Flight Research Center pp. 15,
20; NASA/Johnson Space Center pp. 18, 23, 26;
NASA/Kennedy Space Center title page, pp. 21.
22, 28; Ohio Historical Society pp. 4, 6, 7, 14;
Spanky's Yearbook Archive p. 9

Every effort has been made to contact copyright
holders of any material reproduced in this book.
Any omissions will be rectified in subsequent
printings if notice is given to the publisher.

The photograph of Neil Armstrong on the cover was
taken in 1962.

Contents

Some words are shown in bold, **like this.** You can find out what they mean by looking in the glossary.

First on the Moon

On July 20, 1969, Commander Neil Armstrong coasted above the surface of the Moon searching for a good place to land. The *Eagle*, his spacecraft, was nearly out of fuel. With only seconds to go, Armstrong found a smooth spot and landed the *Eagle*. Then he put on his space suit and backed down the *Eagle*'s ladder. Half a billion people watched on their televisions as Neil Armstrong became the first person in history to touch the Moon.

Neil Armstrong is about three years old here.

Timeline

1930	1946	1950	1955	1956
Born in Wapakoneta, Ohio	*Earns pilot license*	*Fights in Korean War*	*Graduates from Purdue University*	*Marries Janet Shearon; enters astronaut program*

Neil's first airplane ride was in a plane similar to this one.

Neil Alden Armstrong had spent years preparing for that moment. He was born on August 5, 1930, in Wapakoneta, Ohio. He was only two when his parents took him to watch the Cleveland Air Races. At age six, he took his first plane ride in a Ford Tri-Motor Airplane. Neil Armstrong was hooked on flying. In first grade, he read nearly 100 books, and many were about flying.

1966	1969	1971	1986
Commands Gemini 8	Commands Apollo 11; walked on the Moon	Teaches at University of Cincinnati	Serves on Challenger commission

5

Childhood

Neil's family moved often because of his father Stephen Armstrong's job. By the time Neil was thirteen, he had attended school in five different Ohio towns.

Neil's mother, Viola, read to Neil, his sister June, and his brother Dean. The Armstrongs attended church every Sunday. Neil made many friends. He joined the Boy Scouts and the school band. He played a horn and formed a small jazz band. He also took piano lessons.

Neil Armstrong is pushing his sister June on a tricycle.

Neil is dressed in his band uniform.

Neil spent much of his time dreaming about flying. He used a neighbor's **telescope** to explore the sky. Because he planned to be an airplane designer when he grew up, he studied drawings of planes and built models. He hung them from the ceiling of his room. Years later, when he was an astronaut, he still had some of the models he had made as a boy.

Flying

In 1943, when Neil was beginning high school, the family returned to Wapakoneta. Neil wanted to fly. He found an after-school job in a drugstore so that he could pay for flying lessons at a local airfield. During the next few years, Neil earned flying money by working in a bakery, in a grocery store, and doing odd jobs for the pilots.

Neil was only fifteen when he learned to fly in a plane like this one.

This is Neil Armstrong's high school graduation picture.

Neil learned to fly in a few months, but he had to wait until he turned sixteen to get a pilot's **license.** On his birthday, August 5, 1946, Neil took his first **solo** flight and earned his pilot's license. Even though he was excited, he did not tell his friends about his new license.

College

Purdue University is located in West Lafayette, Indiana.

Neil planned to study **aeronautical engineering** in college. Because his family was not rich, he applied to a special Navy program to help pay for college. Neil was excited to learn that he had been accepted. The government would pay his college costs if he agreed to work for the Navy for three years. Neil agreed. He began classes at Purdue University in 1947.

This map shows the area where the Korean War took place.

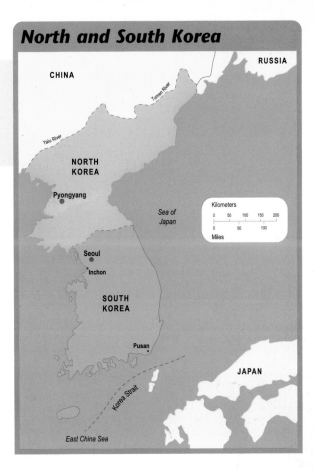

North and South Korea

Neil took science, math, and aeronautical engineering classes. Aeronautical engineering taught him how airplanes work and how to design and build them. Even though Neil did well and enjoyed college, he had to leave Purdue in 1949 to attend Navy flight school in Florida. Fighting had begun in Korea, and the Navy needed pilots. Neil's scholarship required him to report for Navy service whenever his country needed him.

Korean War

The Korean War (1950–1953) was between North and South Korea. The United States fought with the South Koreans against the North Koreans.

Combat Pilot

At Navy flight school, Neil learned how to land an airplane on a ship called an **aircraft carrier.** Then he went to Texas to learn to fly F8F Bearcats and the newest Navy plane, the F9F Panther jet. Neil was only twenty, but he was flying the world's fastest planes. He left for Korea in 1950. He was assigned to the U.S.S. *Essex,* an aircraft carrier.

This Navy photograph shows propeller and jet fighters like the ones Armstrong flew.

Neil Armstrong is buckled into the pilot's seat during training.

During the Korean War, Neil flew 78 combat missions. He earned three medals for his courage and bravery. As soon as the U.S.S. *Essex* reached home, Neil left the Navy and headed back to Purdue to finish his college education. At Purdue he met Janet Shearon, who was also a student there. They enjoyed spending time together, and soon fell in love.

Test Pilot

In 1955, Neil graduated from Purdue University. He began doing research into how jets fly at a laboratory in Cleveland, Ohio. Later that same year, he moved to Edwards Air Force Base in California to become a test pilot.

In January 1956, Neil married Janet Shearon. They settled into a mountain cabin and had fun fixing it up. Their son, Eric, was born in 1957, and their daughter Karen was born in 1959.

Mr. and Mrs. Neil Armstrong celebrate their wedding.

Armstrong prepares for a test flight in the X-15.

In 1959, Armstrong began testing a new kind of plane, an X-15. The X-15 had a rocket engine and could travel at seven times the speed of sound. Armstrong flew over 1,000 hours testing the X-15. He proved that he was one of the best test pilots flying. He knew how to control a plane, and he could keep calm even in scary situations. When **NASA** announced that it was looking for astronauts, Neil Armstrong applied.

Astronaut

Armstrong, his wife, and two-year-old son, Mark, leave an airfield in Houston.

Armstrong passed the required tests with high scores. He was one of nine astronauts chosen for Project Gemini. Unlike most other astronauts who were members of the military, Neil Armstrong was a **civilian.**

In 1962, the Armstrongs moved to Houston, Texas. Their son, Mark, was born the next year.

Project Gemini

Project Gemini was named for the Latin word for twins. The Gemini space capsule was big enough for two men. Project Gemini would test the effects of long trips into space and help prepare the way for a Moon landing.

This simulator prepared astronauts for the twisting and turning of space flight.

Astronauts used **simulators,** or models of space vehicles, to train for space flight. Armstrong helped to make the simulators as close to the real thing as possible so that astronauts would be prepared for their space missions. In 1965, Armstrong trained as a backup pilot for *Gemini 5*. If the astronaut Gordon Cooper could not make the trip, Armstrong would. Cooper flew the mission, but the training helped prepare Armstrong for his own flight.

Gemini 8

Finally, in 1966, Armstrong and another astronaut, David Scott, were assigned to fly *Gemini 8*. They practiced **docking,** or meeting and connecting, with the Agena rocket. A Moon landing vehicle would have to dock with the space ship so that the astronauts could return to Earth.

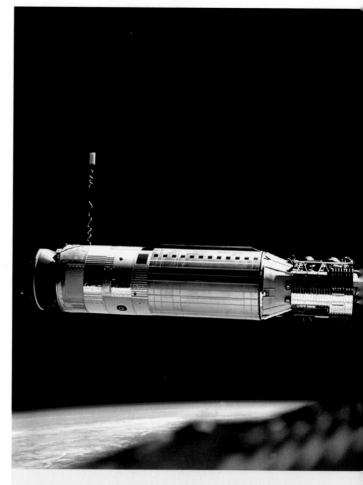

Gemini 8 docked with the Agena rocket. This picture was taken from *Gemini 8*.

On March 16, 1966, the Agena rocket blasted into space. *Gemini 8* followed. Five hours later Armstrong and Scott docked *Gemini 8* with the rocket. At first, it seemed perfect.

Thirty minutes later, *Gemini 8* and the Agena began to spin. Armstrong tried to stop the spinning. As *Gemini 8* spun faster and faster, the astronauts got dizzy. If they kept spinning, the astronauts would **black out.** Armstrong worked fast. He shut down the thrusters that powered *Gemini 8*. It took him thirty minutes to stop the spinning, but his quick thinking saved the astronauts' lives. They landed in the Pacific Ocean ten hours after they lifted off.

Armstrong and Scott crash landed in the Pacific. Here, rescuers help them out of *Gemini 8*.

Apollo 11

NASA scientists and astronauts used the information from the Gemini flights to plan for a Moon landing. The Apollo program was designed to send three men into space and finally to the Moon by 1970. Armstrong began training for the Moon landing.

In January 1969, NASA assigned Neil Armstrong, Buzz Aldrin, and Michael Collins to *Apollo 11*. Armstrong was named flight commander.

This **simulator**, called the Flying Bedstead, trained astronauts to land on the Moon.

Armstrong, Collins, and Aldrin peek out of the *Apollo 11* command module during an equipment check.

After years of planning and testing, *Apollo 11* was headed for the Moon! Armstrong worked ten to twelve hours a day to make sure every detail of the mission was correct. Finally, they were ready. They named the **command module** *Columbia* in honor of the voyage of Christopher Columbus, and the **lunar module** *Eagle,* in honor of the United States.

Neil Armstrong Firsts

- *First **civilian** astronaut*
- *First person to step onto the moon*

Landing on the Moon

This is NASA's official photograph of the *Apollo 11* crew: Armstrong (left), Collins, and Aldrin.

At 9:32 A.M. on July 16, 1969, *Apollo 11* blasted into space. On July 19 it reached **Moon orbit.** Armstrong and Aldrin crawled through a tunnel into the *Eagle* **lunar module,** turned on the computers, and checked the systems. They put on their space suits and prepared to separate from the *Columbia.* The *Eagle* pulled away from *Columbia* with Armstrong and Aldrin inside. Michael Collins remained in *Columbia* orbiting the Moon. Armstrong and Aldrin watched the Moon's surface getting closer and closer.

Warning lights went off, but **NASA** told them to keep going. Armstrong noticed that the *Eagle* was headed toward a rocky field. He took control and guided *Eagle* to a safe landing site. Armstrong and Aldrin were eager to explore, but first they ate and put on their space suits. The space suits would give them oxygen and drinking water, and would keep their bodies at a safe temperature.

Eagle, the lunar module, is shown here in a photograph taken by Michael Collins. Armstrong and Aldrin were inside.

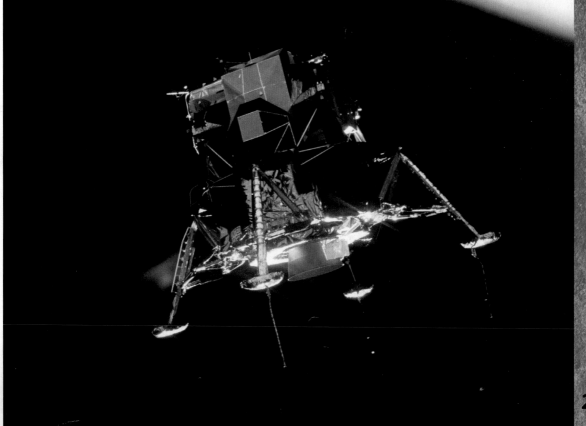

First Small Step

Armstrong climbed out of *Eagle* first. He backed down a ladder to the Moon's surface. On the way, he turned on a camera to record the adventure. At 10:56 P.M. Neil Armstrong became the first person in history to step onto the Moon.

Half a billion people heard Armstrong's first words from the surface of the moon: *"That's one small step for man, one giant leap for mankind."*

Neil Armstrong took this picture of Aldrin walking on the moon during their lunar landing. Armstrong can be seen in the helmet's reflection.

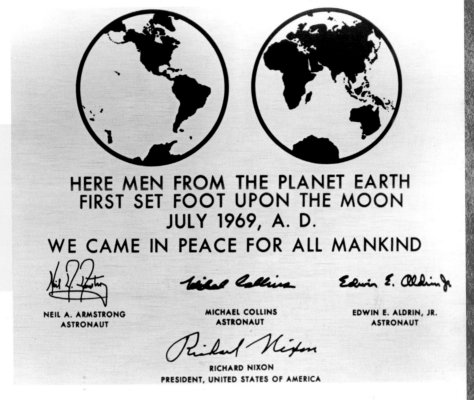

This is a copy of the plaque left on the Moon.

HERE MEN FROM THE PLANET EARTH
FIRST SET FOOT UPON THE MOON
JULY 1969, A. D.
WE CAME IN PEACE FOR ALL MANKIND

NEIL A. ARMSTRONG
ASTRONAUT

MICHAEL COLLINS
ASTRONAUT

EDWIN E. ALDRIN, JR.
ASTRONAUT

RICHARD NIXON
PRESIDENT, UNITED STATES OF AMERICA

Buzz Aldrin followed Armstrong to the surface. The astronauts took pictures of the Moon and of each other. Then they began setting up experiments so that Earth's scientists could learn about the Moon. They collected Moon rocks, left a **plaque** on the Moon's surface, and set up a United States flag. All too soon, it was time to get back into the **lunar module** and **dock** with *Columbia*.

Moon Message

The Apollo 11 plaque tells of how the astronauts came in the spirit of peace.

Fame

The *Eagle* had no trouble **docking** with *Columbia*. After a happy greeting from Michael Collins, the astronauts began the trip back to Earth. On July 24, they splashed down in the Pacific Ocean. Because scientists feared that the astronauts might have picked up germs on the Moon, they kept

President Nixon greets the astronauts, who are still in isolation.

the astronauts away from other people for eighteen days. No one got sick, and on August 11, 1969, the astronauts returned to their families. They were heroes. Everyone wanted to see them.

The astronauts attended parades in New York, Washington, D.C., Chicago, and other cities. They spoke to the United States Congress. They toured the world and met kings, queens, and world leaders. They spoke to hundreds of people and received awards of all kinds. Everywhere they went, people wanted to talk with and touch the men who walked on the Moon.

Ohio, Home of Astronauts

There are more astronauts from Ohio than from any other state.

New York City welcomes the astronauts with a parade. Armstrong is on the right, Aldrin in the middle, and Collins on the left.

Life out of the Spotlight

Neil Armstrong had always been a private person. He did not enjoy all the attention and fame that the Moon walk brought to him. He worked for **NASA** in Washington, D.C., until 1971. After leaving NASA, Armstrong returned to Ohio where he taught **engineering** at the University of Cincinnati for almost ten years. In 1980, Armstrong bought a 200-acre dairy farm in Lebanon, Ohio. He also worked with several engineering companies.

Collins took this photo of the lunar module returning from the surface of the Moon. Half of Earth is visible in the background.

Armstrong (shown here, left), Aldrin, and Collins met with President George W. Bush in 2004 to celebrate the 35th anniversary of their lunar landing.

In 1986, when the space shuttle *Challenger* exploded, Armstrong served on a special **presidential commission** to study the cause of the explosion. The commission said the explosion was caused by cold weather and equipment problems. NASA engineers **redesigned** the equipment.

Neil Armstrong still lives in Ohio and dreams about space travel and the wonders of space. His walk on the Moon was a giant step for mankind. Like other explorers, Armstrong took a great risk and helped us to better understand our world.

Glossary

aeronautical engineering   the science of planning and design of flying machines

aircraft carrier   ship designed to carry airplanes

black out   lose consciousness

civilian   person who is not a member of the military or police

command module   main part of the spaceship carrying the astronauts

dock   meet or connect spacecraft while in space

engineering   science of planning and designing

license   written permission to do something

lunar module   spacecraft designed to land on the Moon

Moon orbit   move in a circle around the Moon

NASA   National Aeronautics and Space Administration, the agency that studies and carries out work in space

plaque   engraved or ornamental sign

presidential commission   committee set up by the president

redesign   make better

reunion   meet again

simulator   model of a space vehicle used in training

solo   by oneself

telescope   instrument that makes the stars seem nearer

More Books to Read

Bramley, Franklyn M. *Mission to Mars*. New York: HarperCollins, 2002.

Brown, Don. *One Giant Leap: The Story of Neil Armstrong*. Boston: Houghton Mifflin, 1998.

Goldsmith, Mike. *Neil Armstrong: The First Man on the Moon*. Austin: Raintree Steck-Vaughn, 2001.

Zemlicka, Shannon. *Neil Armstrong*. Minneapolis: Lerner, 2003.

Places to Visit

Neil Armstrong Air and Space Museum
500 South Apollo Drive
Wapakoneta, Ohio 45895-0978
Phone: 419-738-8811 or 1-800-BUCKEYE

National Air and Space Museum
Independence Ave at 4th Street, SW
Washington, D.C. 20560
Phone: 202-633-1000

Index